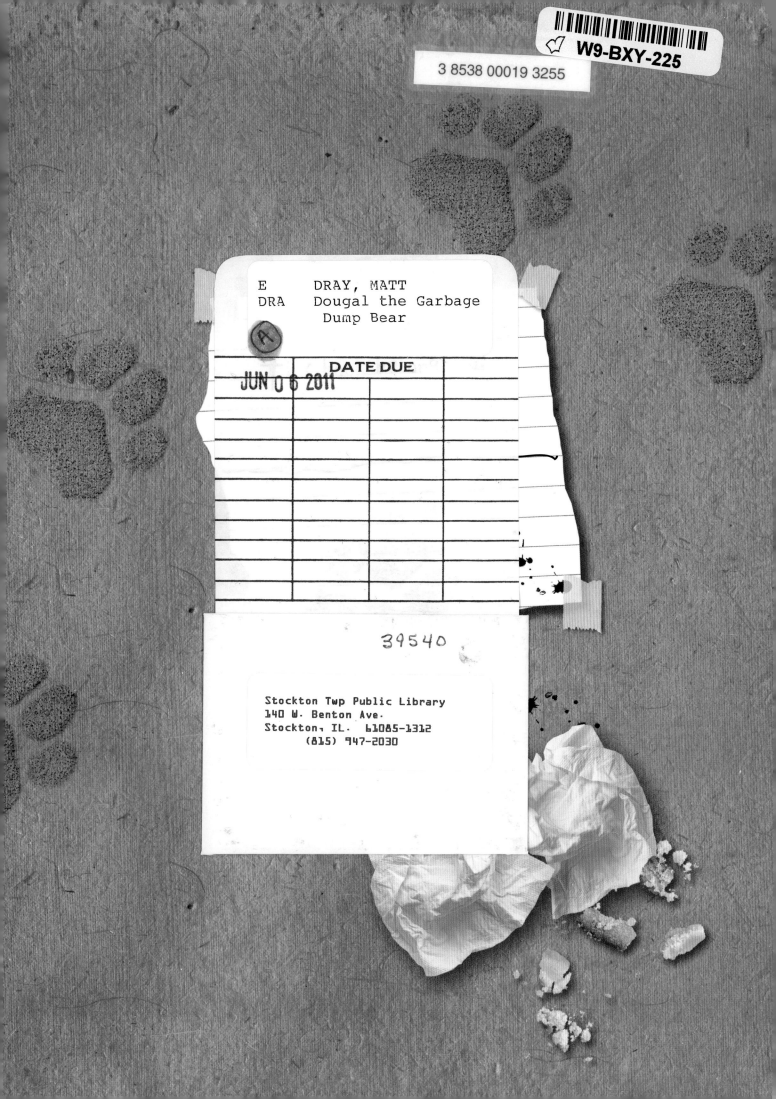

DOUGAL THE GARBAGE DUMP BEAR

To Mum and Dad

matt dray

Kane/Miller
BOOK PUBLISHERS

Dougal was found at a garbage dump on the Gold Coast by Matt Dray in 2002.
All the other dump toys, except for Big Bear, were found there also. Big Bear was brought
to the dump courtesy of Ed Newman. The tea party toys were supplied courtesy of
Elysse Cornford. The dragon ended up on its side courtesy of Matt.

Matt Dray no longer works at the dump.

First American Edition 2005
by Kane/Miller Book Publishers, Inc.
La Jolla, California

Copyright © Matt Dray, 2004

First published in Australia in 2004 by
Penguin Group (Australia)

Cover and text design by Debra Billson © Penguin Group (Australia)

Library of Congress Control Number: 2005921367

Printed and Bound in China by Regent Publishing Services Ltd.
1 2 3 4 5 6 7 8 9 10

ISBN 1-929132-78-6

The author has donated part of his proceeds from this book to the Leukaemia Foundation of
Australia. The Foundation is dedicated to the care of patients and their families and also funds
research into cures and better treatments for leukaemia and related blood disorders. For further
information on the Leukaemia Foundation's work please visit www.leukaemia.com

Dougal

Dougal was a shy little bear with a heart of gold.
He never got to play with the other toys in the
house because they were all new and clean and
perfect and he was not.

He often wished he could be new like them, especially
the day the little girl who owned all the toys
had a tea party.

It was a lovely party. They had patty cakes and ginger-nut biscuits and little triangular peanut butter sandwiches and strawberry milk.

They all sang a song, Pinky Pig told some jokes and Mr. and Mrs. Bunny brought along their new baby girl to show everyone. But no one spoke to Dougal. He sat quietly on his own and ate his cake.

Pinky   Mr. and Mrs. Bunny

Just as the party was finishing, it began to rain, and the little girl had to hurry and put all the toys inside before they got wet. She took the best toys in first; and by the time it got to Dougal's turn it was raining so hard and he was already so wet, she decided not to bother.

So Dougal stayed out in the rain on his own all night. The next morning, the little girl's father found Dougal still sitting at the table. He was soaking wet.

"This bear's no good anymore," said her father.
So he put Dougal in the bin.

Dougal didn't like the bin. It was very smelly.
He hoped the little girl would come and save him,
but she never did.

Early the next morning, Dougal heard the sound of a truck. It stopped right next to the bin. Suddenly, Dougal and the bin were picked up, and he was tipped with all the other rubbish into the truck.

Then it drove away. Every time it stopped, more rubbish would pour in on top of Dougal. Then the truck drove for a long time. When it stopped again, the back end opened up and Dougal was pushed out onto the ground with all the rubbish.

Dougal blinked his eyes
in the sunshine and wondered
where he was.

All of a sudden, there was a loud roar.
The ground shook, and a great big tractor with steel
wheels rumbled past. It just missed Dougal's head.

Then a scary-looking machine with steel tracks
and a huge mouth came straight for him.

It was so big and loud and bellowed so much
smoke that Dougal thought it was a dragon.
The dragon was so close now that Dougal was
frightened he was going to be squashed. But just
as it was about to flatten him, the dragon stopped.

A man hopped out of the cab and picked Dougal up.
He sat the little bear on the ground, out of harm's
way, and then went back to work. Dougal sat there
for the rest of the day and watched the dragon
and the big tractor and the trucks do their work.

At the end of the day, the man put Dougal in the cab of the big tractor. "See you tomorrow," said the man. Dougal didn't want to be left alone again, but it was warm and quiet in the tractor and after a while he felt safe.

The next day, the man found a bench for Dougal and sat him on it so he wouldn't be run over.

One morning, about two weeks later, Dougal was sitting on his bench when he heard a funny voice say, "To bee, or not to bee."

He turned around and saw a bee sitting on a log.

"Hello," said Dougal.

"Hello," said the bee. "What is this place? Mars?"

"It's a garbage dump," said Dougal.

The bee looked around. "That'd bee right. Just my luck."

"I'm Dougal," said Dougal.

"I'm Bumble," said the bee. "Pleased to meet you, Dougal. Shame it's not a better spot."

"It's not bad once you get used to it," said Dougal.

They sat together and watched the machines at work.

Not long afterwards, the men came over and had lunch with them. They had vegemite sandwiches and cakes and an apple each and iced coffee. "You're right, Dougal," said Bumble. "It's not such a bad place here, is it?"

*B*umble and Dougal became good friends. They had heaps of fun together. Some days they would go down to the pond at the front gate and watch the ducks.

Some days they would watch the trucks.

Some days it was very hot. "Bloomin' heat," Bumble would say, and they would ride in the cab of the dragon because it was air conditioned.

Some days it would rain and it was Dougal and Bumble's job to check the rain gauge. "Bloomin' rain," Bumble would say.

And some days, mostly on fridays, they would go out with the men after work and play pool and get home very late.

Ginger beer

And always the next day, they would both feel very sick from drinking too many ginger beers, and have to sleep it off in the air-conditioned dragon.
"Never again," Bumble would say.
"I need an iced coffee," Dougal would say.

One morning, when Dougal and Bumble were down at the pond watching the ducks, they heard a terrible crash.
"What was that?" asked Dougal.
"I've no idea what it could bee," said Bumble.

They both went back up to the top of the dump to see what had made the noise. When they got there they couldn't believe their eyes. "Blimey!" said Bumble.

The dragon had tipped over on its side. It wasn't making any noise or smoke.
"Poor old dragon," said Dougal. "Don't worry. We'll look after you."

They stayed with the dragon while the men went to get a crane to lift it up.

When the crane came, Bumble and Dougal watched the men put chains around the dragon.
"Bee careful," said Bumble. "Don't break that air conditioner."

After the crane had lifted it up, the men took the dragon down to the workshop to fix it. The dragon was sick for a couple of days, but when it came back it was as good as new.

It was so grateful to Dougal and Bumble for helping that it pushed the garbage much more carefully, so any other toys who came to the dump could be saved.
And they saved heaps.

They saved . . .

7 little bears

2 dogs

11 middle-sized bears

one big bear
and his little brother

2 elephants

2 toucans

2 lemurs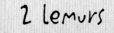

a white tiger and
a scottish moose

5 rabbits

a blue fox
and a red mouse

a clown and
his girlfriend

a koala named Eric

a little doll named Honey
and a gorilla named Gus . . .

. . . and a shaggy thing with one
eye that didn't know what it was,
but they let it stay anyway.

However, forty-five toys could not all live on one
bench, so the men let them stay down near the pond.
"As long as we all bee-have ourselves," Bumble told
the other toys.
"And don't scare the ducks," said Dougal.

All the toys loved their new home. But one day, the big boss came down from the city. He saw all the bears and rabbits and dogs and elephants and the rest, and said, "This is a dump, not a zoo. They have to go."

All the toys were worried.
"What's going to happen to us, Dougal?" they asked.
"Bloomin' big boss," buzzed Bumble. "Why can't he just let us bee?"

When Saturday came, the men piled all the toys into a truck. Dougal didn't want to leave. He'd miss the ducks and the pond and the dragon and the iced coffees.

Pond

Then they drove away.

The man with the truck took the toys back to his house.

It was a lovely little house right on the beach. They couldn't believe their luck.

House

Beach

There was a toy car and a toy motorbike,

and pails and shovels for the beach.

They had a swing set and a climbing castle as well.

There was also
a trampoline,

and when Big Bear bounced he sent all the other
toys flying, and they thought it was great fun.
And then they found out . . .

. . . that Shaggy Thing with One Eye
was a really good surfer.

Every Monday and Friday, the man would take
Dougal and Bumble back to the dump for a visit.

Bumble would ride
in the dragon.

And the man would give Dougal some bread so he could feed the ducks.

And while he sat there on his own, Dougal would think how lucky he was. He remembered how he had been left out in the rain and put in the bin, and he realized that sometimes bad things happen so that good things can happen.

You just had to make the best of it.

THE END